For my grandparents
Mary Eliza and Wilfred Ephraim Solomon

With a special sparkling thank you
to Sue, Molly and Judith

First published in paperback in Great Britain by Collins Picture Books in 2003
This edition published by HarperCollins Children's Books in 2004

1 3 5 7 9 10 8 6 4 2

ISBN: 0 00 719229 0

Collins Picture Books and HarperCollins Children's Books are divisions of HarperCollins Publishers Ltd.
Text and illustrations copyright © Mandy Stanley 2003
The author/illustrator asserts the moral right to be identified as the author/illustrator of the work.
A CIP catalogue record for this title is available from the British Library. All rights reserved. No part of this
publication may be reproduced, stored in a retrieval system or transmitted in any form or by any means,
electronic, mechanical, photocopying, recording or otherwise, without the prior permission of
HarperCollins Publishers Ltd, 77-85 Fulham Palace Road, Hammersmith, London W6 8JB.

Visit our website at:
www.harpercollinschildrensbooks.co.uk

Printed in Hong Kong by Printing Express Ltd.

Lettice

A Christmas Wish
Mandy Stanley

HarperCollins *Children's Books*

Lettice Rabbit and her family lived high up on top of the hill. Nibble, nibble, hop, hop, every day was the same...

until one cold winter's morning. Lettice peeped out of her burrow to find that the world had turned sparkly white...

'Snow!' squeaked Lettice. 'I've never
seen so much snow.' And she put out
a paw to taste it. But as she leaned out
of her burrow, she slipped…

and tumbled...
over and over...
down towards the pond.
'Heeelp!' shrieked Lettice.

BUMP!
She landed flat on her nose
in the middle of the pond.
It was frozen solid.
As she tried to stand...

she slipped
and skidded...

twizzled and
twirled...

just like an
ice skater.

'Wheee! This is fun,'
Lettice giggled.

Suddenly she stopped.
She could hear voices.

Peeping over the bank, Lettice saw some children.
They were having a wonderful time playing in the

snow and collecting things on their toboggan.
'I wonder what they're doing?' thought Lettice.

'Let's go!' called one of the children.
  'Can we finish the Christmas decorations
when we get home?' replied another.

'Christmas!' thought Lettice. 'I've always wanted to know what Christmas is. I'm going to follow them and find out.'

When the children got home they hung
some holly on the front door.

Without them noticing, Lettice slipped
into the house.

Mmm. Something smelled delicious.
  'Biscuits!' yelled the children.
  'But biscuits aren't Christmas,' thought
Lettice, and she hopped into the next
room to explore.

Lettice gasped.

In front of her was a glittering tree, covered with glowing jewels and gold and silver sparkles.

'So this is Christmas!' she whispered, hopping closer. Underneath the tree she saw the best thing of all. A gorgeous fairy doll!

Lettice gently took it out of its box.

'I wish I could be a fairy!' she sighed.

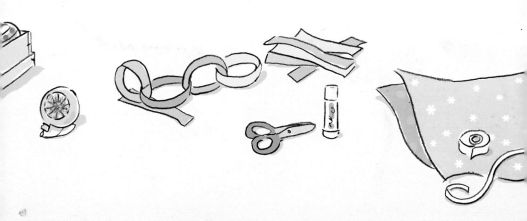

Just then, the children came into the room...

and happily pulled things out of boxes to put on to the tree.

'But where is the fairy?' said one. 'She's gone!'

'Look what I've found!' said the boy.

'A rabbit!' squealed the children with delight.
'What are you doing here?'

'I just wanted to find out about Christmas,'
blushed Lettice.

'Christmas is about decorating the house and being with the people we love,' said the girl.

'And Father Christmas brings us presents!' said the boy.

'And all our wishes come true,'
said the other little girl.

'I have a Christmas wish,' sighed Lettice.
'I wish I could be a Christmas fairy.'

The children clapped their hands. 'That's easy!'

They made Lettice
a fairy dress,

little sparkly slippers,

and fairy wings made
of tissue and tinsel.

When Lettice saw
her reflection,
she couldn't
believe her eyes.
'I really am a
Christmas fairy.'

Lettice wanted to tell her brothers and sisters all about Christmas.

'We'll take you home on our toboggan,' said the children.

When it was time to say goodbye they gave Lettice a beautiful box.

'Merry Christmas, Lettice!' they cried.

'Oh! Thank you!' cried Lettice and she raced into the burrow.

'Where have you been?' cried all her family.
  'I've been to find Christmas,' she said,
opening the box. 'Follow me, I know just
what to do with these!'

Lettice and her brothers and sisters hung the shiny decorations on the tree outside their burrow. The little Christmas tree shimmered and twinkled in the moonlight.

Lettice was so happy, it felt like magic had
come to their burrow that night.
'Merry Christmas, everyone,'
she called.
    Merry Christmas, Lettice.